Attack!

Written by
Jeanne Gowen Dennis and Sheila Seifert

Cover illustration by David Hohn
Interior illustrations by Ron Adair

www.cookcommunications.com/kidz

Faith
Building
Guide

Ages
9 and up

Obedience

Faith Kidz® is an imprint of Cook Communications Ministries
Colorado Springs, Colorado 80918
Cook Communications, Paris, Ontario
Kingsway Communications, Eastbourne, England

ATTACK!
©2003 by Jeanne Gowen Dennis and Sheila Seifert

First printing, 2003
Printed in U.S.A.
1 2 3 4 5 6 7 8 9 10 Printing/Year 07 06 05 04 03

Senior Editor: Heather Gemmen
Design Manager: Jeffrey P. Barnes
Designer: Granite Design

For my Sunday school kids. Praise the Lord in song, and let God fight your battles. –JGD

For Tyler, Kaitlyn, and Amanda Dreman. –SS

Special thanks to Heather Gemmen for letting us develop her idea into a series of adventures and to Mary McNeil for recommending us.

Have you ever wanted to witness the Red Sea opening or the walls of Jericho falling? The Strive to Survive series takes you into the middle of the action of your favorite Bible stories.

In each story, you are the main character. What happens is up to you! Through your choices, you can receive great rewards, get into big trouble, or even lose your life.

Your goal is to choose well and survive.
Your adventure begins now.

Attack!

A warm breeze makes your tunic flutter as you stand on a grassy hillside near Judah's border. When the enemy comes, you will be ready. You swallow the last chunk of bread from the leather pouch at your side. The peaceful bleating of your family's sheep makes it hard to believe that war could break out soon. Three armies, including the neighboring Edomites, plan to attack—at least that's what you've heard.

You choose several smooth stones for your sling. With God's help, you're sure to beat the enemy, just as King David did almost one hundred years ago when he killed Goliath.

Was that a noise? It sounded like someone stepping on loose stones. You study the rocks and plants on the hillside across from you. Was that movement in the distance?

Your heart races and your throat tightens. You don't know if you're ready to fight the enemy all by yourself. Everything is silent. You are afraid even to breathe. Suddenly, something leaps from behind a boulder. Whew! It was only a rabbit.

You fill your scrip—the leather pouch that held
your lunch—with rocks. Then you sit down. Maybe
it is silly to worry about the enemy. You live in
such a little town; they probably won't even bother
to attack here. You pick up your kinnor and gently
strum it. Your great-grandfather played this u-shap-
ed harp in the Temple of Jerusalem when Solomon
was king. You have just begun to sing one of
David's psalms when suddenly two strong arms pull
you backward. Other arms tear your instrument
from you.

You cringe, waiting to die, until you see the
faces of Joash and his friends. You try to pull away
from them, but their arms hold you tightly.

"Stop it!" you yell. One of the boys has your
kinnor. "Give it back!"

Joash jumps on top of you and sits on your
stomach. He is bigger and stronger. Your back is
pressed against sharp rocks, and your eyes look up
into a blue-gray sky.

"Some watcher you are. You didn't even hear
us coming," Joash says.

One of Joash's friends sneers, "And you were
scared of a tiny rabbit."

"I was not," you say. "I was just—"

Joash covers your mouth with his hands. "We
saw you jump. You're too much of a baby to protect sheep. Your father just sends you out here so

no one will have to listen to your squeaky voice or the awful music you make." Joash smells worse than the dirt-caked wool on your sheep.

His friends toss your kinnor back and forth between them. You don't want them to break it, but you can't say anything with Joash's stinky hand in your face.

"You're not even worth fighting." Joash pushes his weight down on you as he stands up.

"Just wait until the attack comes," you say, sitting up. "I'll fight for Judah as hard as the bravest soldier."

"You? You're too scrawny to hold a real weapon."

You roll to the side and grab your rod to hit Joash, but as soon as it is in your hand, one of his friends kicks it to the ground. You hate how helpless they make you feel.

"You can't even handle a rod," Joash taunts. "All you're good for is watching tame sheep." He laughs. "What an ugly instrument." He takes your kinnor from the others and tosses it high into the air.

"Don't! That belongs to my family," you yell. "Give it back now or I'll tell my father."

Joash smiles. "If you want your old harp, come and get it." He and his friends run down the other side of the hill, throwing it wildly between them. You feel the blood rising in your face and breathe deeply to keep from yelling the wrong words after them.

You want your kinnor back, but you are supposed to be watching the sheep. Your brother is going to relieve you soon. A figure in the distance looks like it could be Reuben, but you can't be certain.

CHOICE ONE: If you wave to the person in the distance and then chase after Joash, go to page 9.

CHOICE TWO: If you stay with the sheep and then later tell your parents what happened, go to page 11.

CHOICE THREE: If you follow the bullies while trying to keep an eye on your sheep, go to page 14.

You stare into the distance. The person is wearing a light colored robe like your brother's, and his hair is dark. "It has to be Reuben," you think. You wave your hands in the air in a large circle. When you feel certain that Reuben sees you, you tie up your robe and run after Joash and his friends.

They head over the ridge. Instead of running directly after them, you take a shortcut and skirt the hills to cut them off. A pebble slides into your sandal, but you can't stop to remove it. Timing is everything. You would rather ignore the sharp lump under your arch if it means you will get your kinnor back.

The sound of laughter and scuffling feet to your left tell you that you were right. They are heading toward the caves. From a cleft in the rock, you jump out. Joash looks startled. "Where did you come from?" Without a word, you lunge at the kinnor. Thinking quickly, Joash steps to the side. Your fingers grab empty air. Off balance, you fall to the hard ground. As your head hits the dirt, the jolt makes you bite your lip.

Ignoring the taste of blood, you say, "Give it back!"

"Come and get it!" Joash yells, tossing it to a friend.

One of them says, "This way!" You stand up as they slide down the hill to a cave. Their laughter echoes as they go inside. You hurry to the cave entrance, where the air smells stale and feels stagnant.

CHOICE ONE: If you follow them into the cave, go to page 16.

CHOICE TWO: If you mark the cave to find it later and then hurry back to the sheep, go to page 19.

Although you are afraid that you will never see your kinnor again, you do not run after Joash. You must stay with the sheep. Your family is depending on you to keep them safe. When the person in the distance disappears in another direction, you are glad you did not mistake the traveler for Reuben. By the time Reuben gets to you, Joash is long gone.

That night over a meal of vegetables and barley bread, you tell your parents what happened. When you are finished eating, they take you to Joash's house. You knock on the wooden door. Joash's father fills the doorway.

Your father says, "Pardon the intrusion, but our child accuses your son of stealing our family's kinnor."

You can't wait for Joash to get what he deserves. You can smell lentil stew in the air as you are invited inside. They probably just finished cleaning up after their evening meal.

"Joash, come here," his father says. "Did you take this family's kinnor?" Joash shakes his head no. He puts on a humble expression. You feel like hitting him.

"No, father," he says. "I was with the Rabbi all day. My friends were with me. They will tell you."

Your father smiles apologetically. "We are sorry to have disturbed you." You can't believe that your father would give up so easily.

Your father's smile tightens, and you know you

should not speak. But when you are away from Joash's house, you say, "He did take my kinnor." Your father remains silent. It is a quiet walk back to your house.

Once inside, your father says, "You lost it, didn't you? We told you over and over to be careful with that kinnor. I should have waited to give it to you until you were older and more responsible."

"Is it possible that you broke the kinnor and are afraid to tell us?" your mother asks. "Don't be afraid to tell the truth. Lying is much worse than a broken kinnor. Once when I was a girl, I broke my mother's favorite bowl and then made up a tale about how it was stolen. The lies kept growing until I was eventually found out."

"I didn't lose or break it," you say. "Joash stole it."

"I want the truth from you," your father says.

"I am telling the truth."

Your mother looks at you sadly and sighs. "We are glad that you stayed with the sheep."

Your parents stop talking about the kinnor, but you can tell that they think you lied to them. You are so angry that they are taking Joash's word over yours that you decide to run away.

CHOICE ONE: If you run as fast and as far away as you can go, turn to page 21.

CHOICE TWO: If you hide in the caves for a few days to give your parents a chance to change their minds, go to page 23.

Even as you start to run after Joash, you wonder whether you should be chasing him or watching your sheep. You are torn. You hope you can do both.

"Joash, I'll tell your father if you don't give it back right now!" you yell.

"Tattle-tale!" he calls back. You stub your sandal on the uneven ground.

"If you give it back to me right now," you yell, "I'll take your turn watching your family's sheep." You look back at your sheep to make sure that they are okay. Then you continue the chase.

"You'd only get me into trouble," he yells. He tosses your kinnor to one of his friends. The instrument flying through the air gives a soft whirring sound. His friend catches it and then tosses the kinnor back. The instrument makes an abrupt twang when Joash grabs it. To you, it sounds like a cry for help.

"You are going to be in big trouble if you don't give it to me right now," you yell. You look back at your sheep. They are still okay, but when you can't smell their scent even on the breeze, you know you are too far.

You turn your attention to the boys in time to see Joash throw your kinnor high into the air.

CHOICE ONE: If you sprint and try to catch it, go to page 25.

CHOICE TWO: If you yell at him, go to page 27.

You hurry into the cave so that you won't lose them. The darkness blinds you, and you have to stop to let your eyes get used to your surroundings. As you wait, you listen. You hear dripping water and faint squeaking sounds. You duck out of the way of a sudden fluttering of wings. A cold shiver runs down your spine. You wish you had your cloak.

In the distance, you hear muffled panting and laughter. It seems to be coming from your right. You move farther into the cave, letting your hand trail along the stone edges. The walls feel cool. In some spots, they are damp and almost slimy. You let go of the wall and pull your arms closer to your body.

Something is crawling up your arm. You stifle a scream and brush off the creature. You do not want Joash to know you are following him or that you are scared. Unable to handle the bugs, you spin around to leave, but the thought of a broken kinnor makes you change your mind. With a sigh, you move once again in the direction of the laughter.

Everything is silent now. Just then, something drops on your head. You close your eyes and clench your fists until you feel wetness dripping down your scalp. It is only water. You take a deep breath and proceed, trying not to think about the spiders and other creatures above and all around you.

You turn a sharp corner. A dim shaft of light from above shines directly on an enormous spider in front of you. Your scream echoes through the cave as you duck to get away from it. In your haste, you slip on loose rocks and lose your balance. Your left foot gets wedged between the stones. Other rocks slip around your ankle.

A sharp pain runs up your leg as you try to pull out your foot. It will not budge. The spider hovers above you in the cave's only sliver of dim light. Your skin feels like it is crawling with bugs. Are they real, or are you imagining them? Either way, you have to get out of there fast! You pull harder to free your foot, biting your tunic to keep from yelling in pain. The wool gags you. Your ankle is at a dangerous angle, and you are afraid you will break it if you are not careful.

CHOICE ONE: If you pray and ask God for help, go to page 49.

CHOICE TWO: If you begin yelling for help, go to page 51.

You have to get back to the sheep, so you take a soft stone and mark the cave opening. That way you will be able to find the entrance again and search for your kinnor later tonight.

You hurry back to the field, where the sheep are still grazing. They look so peaceful. Reuben has not yet arrived. The person you saw in the distance must have been a traveler, not your brother. You circle the sheep to warn predators that the flock is under your protection.

When your brother finally comes to relieve you, you hurry home as fast as you can and tell your parents what happened.

Your father says, "We gave you that kinnor because we thought you were old enough to take care of it."

You try to explain. "But Joash and his friends—"

"I am very disappointed in you," your father says. You realize that your father thinks the kinnor is lost forever.

That night, you wait for everyone to fall asleep before you sneak out with a small clay lamp. You are going to find your kinnor! You go to the spot where you think you saw Joash enter the caves, but you can't find your mark. Joash could have entered either of the two caves in front of you.

CHOICE ONE: If you enter the cave entrance on the left, go to page 66.

CHOICE TWO: If you enter the cave entrance on the right, go to page 68.

When your mother is in the house and your father has turned his attention to other things, you casually move toward the road and then boldly walk away from your village. You do not look back. When you have walked for a while, you throw back your head and begin to run. If your family will not believe the truth, maybe strangers will.

You want to get as far away as you can. You run and run as the sky darkens. Although you were tired earlier, you seem to have new strength now. You run for a long time. Tears blind your eyes. You taste their salt streaming into your mouth. You can't see clearly in front of you. Your side aches, but you keep running until you are too exhausted to think. Hours pass in a darkness where only the sound of your breathing reaches your ears.

The air no longer smells familiar, but you do not stop. You keep running. Your emotions carry you forward. The scent in the air grows stronger. You follow it until you see campfires in the distance. You head toward them, hoping to find bread, water, and a warm place to rest. Just in time, you realize that you have happened upon the camp of the Ammonite, Edomite, and Moabite armies. These are the ones getting ready to attack Judah! One of the sentries looks in your direction. You drop to the ground, hoping he didn't see you in the darkness.

He moves toward you with his weapon raised. You slide on your stomach over pebbles and pricker plants to get away from the place where he might have seen you. Each time he stops moving to listen, you lie completely still so that he doesn't hear you move. Prickles are digging into your stomach.

"Stand up, you coward, and come here, or I'll kill you where you lie!" He is looking directly at you.

CHOICE ONE: If you stand up and ask for mercy, go to page 32.

CHOICE TWO: If you stay where you are and do not move, go to page 35.

In the night, you take some of your family's food and your cloak. You go to the caves not far from your village and hide.

"I'll stay away long enough to make them feel sorry for not believing me," you tell yourself. You live in a cave for three days. Finally, you grow tired of being alone. You have eaten all your food. You decide to go home.

When you get back, your village is empty. Everyone is gone. You go from house to house, wondering what has happened. From a neighbor's window, you see foreign soldiers searching other homes. You realize that the rumors of war are true.

You hurry out of the house without stopping to take any food. You ignore your growling stomach, craving only the safety of the caves.

In your haste to get back to the cave, you fall and cut your leg. You stifle your cries of pain to keep the foreigners from discovering you. Fortunately, you are able to make it back to your hiding place without being seen.

Your cut keeps bleeding. You put pressure on it, but it won't stop. You suddenly feel weak from the loss of blood and lack of food. You lie down on your cloak to rest. You fall asleep. When you wake up, a crust of dried blood has formed over your wound, but it throbs and feels hot to the touch.

In the middle of the night, you can't move your leg without it hurting. By morning, you are delirious with fever and can't move to get food or water. The infection in your leg eventually spreads into your blood. One night you fall asleep and never wake up.

THE END

You sprint toward the airborne kinnor. Every muscle in your body is tensed in your effort to reach it before it falls to the ground. You don't know if you can catch it, but you have to try. Your hand stretches up into the air. It's as if the world is moving in slow motion for you. Suddenly, the kinnor stops moving upward and begins falling. You aren't close enough! You are afraid you won't get there in time. Joash's laughter sounds far off and distorted.

You feel yourself leave the ground and fly in the direction of your instrument. And then it happens! The kinnor touches the edge of your hand. You have just enough strength to grab it and pull it close to you before you tumble to the ground. It's safe! You are a little scraped up, but relieved. Your heart pumps fast, and you stay where you are to catch your breath. You look up. Joash is there. For a second, he looks relieved; then his usual taunting look returns.

"You're so lame." He spins around and takes off, catching up with his friends.

Just then, you remember the sheep. You can't see them from where you are. You stand and then race up the hill. You breathe a quick, "Thank you, God," when you see them grazing peacefully.

As you sit and watch the sheep, you jump at every sound. You are afraid that Joash and his followers will come back. You hold your kinnor tightly to your chest. You didn't realize how important it was to you until you almost lost it. It is a precious part of your family's history.

After awhile, you see Joash and his friends coming back.

"What do you want?" you ask, moving away from them.

"We don't want you to play your kinnor or sing out here anymore," Joash says.

His friend adds, "We don't like your squeaky voice."

"And what if I sing anyway?"

Joash's face turns threatening. "Next time, you won't get your kinnor back." He turns to his friends. "We've wasted enough time here. Let's go."

As they run off, you sigh.

CHOICE ONE: If you never sing or play your kinnor in front of Joash again, go to page 89.

CHOICE TWO: If you get back at Joash for bullying you, go to page 90.

The kinnor lands and breaks. Rage fills you, and you completely forget about your sheep. You jump up and run after Joash with your fists raised. He starts running. You chase him for miles without thinking about how tired you are.

Joash stops without warning, and you run into him. You back up to catch your breath and prepare for his assault.

He says, "We're in trouble." He points. You look in the direction where he is pointing and see thousands of foreign-looking tents. They go on for as far as you can see.

Your anger vanishes. "Who are they?" You move closer to Joash.

He shakes his head. "The rumors must be true. How can Judah ever win against an army as big as that?"

"What should we do?" you ask.

"I don't know," Joash says. "You're the smart one. What do you think we should do?"

You try not to look startled at the compliment. "Maybe we can find out their plans and warn Judah."

He nods. "Let's sneak along the ridge that over-looks those tents. They're bigger than the others and probably belong to the leaders."

"Okay." Quietly you begin moving toward the ridge. You mimic Joash's movements, and now you understand why you never heard him coming. Joash is good at staying hidden, and he's as silent as a fox.

When you get to the edge of the ridge, you point to the steep side to show Joash where to go. He nods. You both work your way down, helping each other. A few times, dirt and stones slide down ahead of you. You try to move more carefully.

When you reach the base of the ridge, you hear sentries talking on the other side of a large rock, but you can't quite make out what they are saying. Joash puts his hand up to let you know he's listening. When he gives you the signal, you move to a place where you can whisper together.

Joash says, "The first man wanted to know when they will attack us. He thinks they have plenty of soldiers already. The other one says that they are waiting for another army to join them. What should we do now?"

CHOICE ONE: If you leave to warn your village, go to page 37.

CHOICE TWO: If you stay to find out more about the enemy's plans, go to page 39.

You try to cooperate with the soldier, but his flashing eyes scare you. As his questions become more intense, he puts his face right in front of yours. His breath smells like old garlic and rotten teeth. You remind yourself that he is trying to help you. You just want to go home.

"I don't know anything else," you say. "I've told you everything I know. I'd tell you more if I knew more."

The soldier sits and gazes out into the distance. You wonder what he is thinking. Perhaps it is about his son.

"You have betrayed your country," he says simply. "Traitors don't deserve to live." His words surprise you.

He stands up and draws his sword from its sheath. It gleams in the sunlight.

"Oh no!" you say. "But your son is my age. You said that—"

"I'm a soldier," he says. "I don't have any children. You've betrayed the people you love, so you will betray your enemies."

You whisper, "God, please forgive me," just before the soldier kills you.

THE END

You say, "I won't tell you a thing. The God of Judah is stronger than you and your army, and you will regret the day that you chose to mess with God's people."

"You insignificant brat," the soldier says. He returns his sword to its sheath. "You don't understand the power we have. Just look out there at the many armies."

"And you don't know the power of my God," you say. You close your eyes, expecting to feel his sword strike you.

"Killing you would be too easy," says the soldier. "I'm going to keep you alive as my slave. When you have seen your people destroyed and your God shamed, then I will kill you."

You shrug. You don't want him to know how scared you are. From that time on, you have to fetch and clean and carry things for this soldier. He eats chunks of meat and fresh bread that make your mouth water. You are only allowed to eat whatever scraps he leaves behind. He beats you every day. When the army changes its position, your life is especially hard. You have to carry more than your own weight. Although the man is cruel, you try to honor God by the way you behave toward him.

At night, you remember your family, and you miss them. You are sorry for running away. You dream of home and pray that God will help you return someday.

One morning you wake up to the sound of shouting, scuffling, and screaming. You wonder what the commotion is. You stay in your tent. The battle must have begun. The clank of metal grates on your nerves. You hear a moan just outside the tent, and someone falls against it. You crawl into the middle of the tent, trying to hold your trembling body still with your arms. You wonder why you ever wanted to fight for Judah. This is not the romantic idea you had about the life of a soldier. There are too many sounds of metal scraping metal and groans of pain. It might be your imagination, but the smell of sweat mixed with blood reaches your nostrils.

Finally, you must know what is happening. You pull back the tent flap and hold it in a clenched fist. Fighting soldiers and dead bodies are everywhere. The sun is still low in the morning sky. This could be your chance to escape, but you are afraid to leave the tent.

CHOICE ONE: If you stay in the tent, go to page 92.

CHOICE TWO: If you try to escape, go to page 93.

"I give up!" you yell as you slowly stand up.

"Get over here," the soldier demands roughly.

"I don't have a weapon." You walk slowly toward the man. He is even bigger than you imagined. When you reach him, he pushes you toward the camp.

"Where are you taking me?" you ask.

"Be quiet!" he demands. He forces you toward one of the tents and then tosses you inside. It is empty. You hear voices outside, but they are talking so low that you can't understand what they are saying. You hurry to the back of the goat's-hair-cloth tent and grope at the edges next to the ground. You hope to find a loose area so you can escape, but the entire tent is pegged firmly with tent nails.

When the voices quiet, you dive back to the center of the tent. The soldier ducks to enter, and you see faint rays of the rising sun behind him.

"You are an enemy spy. You must die." His sword scrapes against its sheath as he draws it out.

"Mercy, please!" you cry as you kneel before him. "I don't know anything about spying."

The soldier pauses and gives you a long look. "You are about the age of my son." With a sigh, he slides his sword back into its holder.

As if disgusted with himself, he grabs the back of your clothes and drags you. You keep trying to scramble to your feet. You taste the wool of your tunic in your mouth and remember how lovingly

your mother wove it. You grow angry at the man
for handling it so roughly. His sword clanks as he
walks. When you reach a rise above the camp, he
stops and drops you to the ground.

You raise your head and stare at the enemy
tents before you. They go as far as you can see.
Judah can never defeat this vast army.

"I must kill you," the soldier says, "unless we
can find some way that you can be useful to us.
Can you cook for a thousand men?"

"Uh. No."

"You're too scrawny to carry equipment. There
is nothing you can do. I'll have to kill you," he says.
"I'm sorry."

"Wait!" you exclaim. "There has to be something I can do."

"Are you willing to give us information about
your country and its army?"

You hesitate, thinking about all the people back
in your town. But how can little Judah win against
such a multitude?

The man continues. "Look around you.
Whether you tell us anything or not, we will take
over your country. But if you help us, I might be
able to save your family."

"Like Israel did for Rahab when Jericho fell?"
you ask. You ignore the nagging doubt that reminds
you that God was on Israel's side when Jericho fell.

The soldier shrugs. "I don't know anything

about that. If you join us, you'll save yourself, your family, and maybe your whole village."

CHOICE ONE: If you tell the soldier what he wants to know to save your family, go to page 29.

CHOICE TWO: If you refuse to tell the soldier anything, go to page 30.

You do not move. You barely breathe. You hear footsteps.

"Who are you yelling at?" asks a rough voice.

"I thought I saw something," the soldier says. "It must have been a small animal, or else my mind is playing tricks on me."

"Your shift is over," says the rough voice. "I'll take your place."

You hear footsteps walking away.

You continue moving forward, pushing with your toes. Inch by inch, you crawl to rocks that overlook the camp. There is a tent directly below you and a crevice where you can hide under the shelter of a rock. A trickle of a stream flows through the crevice, and a tiny pool has gathered on a small ledge. The moon shimmers on the water. You drink from the pool and then fall asleep.

You awake when you hear voices. "In two days, we should attack Judah!"

"No!" says another angry voice. "We must wait for the rest of the Moabites to join us. They will be here soon."

"You've been saying that for days!"

Someone taps you on the shoulder. You look up, alarmed. A child is looking down at you. He puts his index finger to his mouth for you to be quiet.

He whispers, "I am a slave at this camp. Come with me. If you stay here, they will find you."

CHOICE ONE: If you go with the slave, go to page 79.

CHOICE TWO: If you run away from the slave, go to page 82.

You motion toward the ridge, and Joash nods his understanding. It takes a long time, but you help each other up the cleft in the ridge. Suddenly, your foot catches a loose stone that tumbles off the ledge. Thinking quickly, Joash catches it before it falls to the ground.

You mouth, "Thanks," to him. He gives you a quick smile.

Just then two sentries come into view below you. Before they look up, you both give one last push to make it over the rim undetected. You lie on top of it, and feel yourself shaking. That was too close.

After you have had a moment to rest, you slowly pick your way through the underbrush, away from the camp. You are surprised at how well you both work together.

Once you are far enough away not to be seen or heard, you say, "We have to warn our village."

"And Jerusalem," Joash adds.

"I'll warn the village," you say.

"And I'll take Jerusalem." Joash adds, "May God be with you."

"And with you," you say. You know that Joash has a lot farther to run than you do. Without another word, you give each other a hug. You are in this together.

You run in different directions. Licking the dirt from your lips, you race for home. By the time you get back to your village, everyone is packing to go to Jerusalem. While you were gone, a messenger from King Jehoshaphat commanded all of Judah to come to Jerusalem to fast and pray for victory over the enemy.

"I've seen the army, and Joash is on his way to Jerusalem," you tell your parents, the elders, and Joash's parents. You answer questions about what you and Joash saw. Your news only makes the villagers move more swiftly. You leave as a group for the city.

For such a large group, you are surprised at how quiet everyone is. Even the children are not talking much. Only the sounds of sheep and goats bleating, with an occasional barking dog, fill the air.

When you get to Jerusalem days later, you see Joash in the distance. You are about to wave to him when you notice that he is wearing a soldier's uniform. You are jealous. You are the one who wanted to fight for Judah.

CHOICE ONE: If you avoid Joash, go to page 42.

CHOICE TWO: If you talk to Joash, go to page 43.

You decide to find out more about the enemy's plans so that you can report them to the king in Jerusalem. As you move closer, you step on a rock and slip. The sound draws the sentries to you.

Joash jumps between you and the sentries.

"Run!" he yells to you. "Run!" He flings himself in their way. You take off before other soldiers arrive. You may be small, but you're quick. After all, you kept up with Joash on the way to this camp. You keep telling yourself that to keep up your courage.

Only once do you glance behind you. Joash's limp body is lying on the ground, and soldiers are chasing you. You can't let him die for nothing. He gave his life to help you get away. You run harder than you have ever run. You do not look back. You breathe deeply from the fresh air around you.

You do not want the enemy to follow you to your village, so you head straight for Jerusalem. Although the enemy stops chasing you once you get deep into Judah's territory, you keep running as if Joash were after you. From all his years of bullying you, he has trained you for this important run. You do not stop until you reach Jerusalem.

"I've just come from the enemy camp. Take me to the king," you gasp. Someone gives you water, and you relish its coolness in your mouth and throat. Once you tell King Jehoshaphat about everything you have seen and about what happened to

Joash, you pass out from exhaustion.

When you wake up, many days have passed. Your parents are with you and Judah's battle is over. Judah has won! Although you are content to be with your family, you will never forget what Joash did for you. You just wish you could have saved his life. You might have become good friends.

THE END

You feel as if you've eaten bitter herbs. You quickly duck behind your parents and smell the dust in your mother's traveling robe. Joash is not your friend. He never was. It was your dream to march beside the army, not his.

If you had chosen to warn Jerusalem instead of the village, you would be with the soldiers now instead of Joash. Whenever you see him in the distance, you turn down a different street. For two days, Joash tries to find you.

Your mother says, "Joash came by again."

Your father says, "Go see Joash. I keep running into him, and he asks about you. We were praying together today. Where were you?"

"I was around," you say with a shrug, but you are determined not to meet with Joash. You duck behind people and hide in stinky animal carts to get away from him.

Before long, you watch as Joash marches into battle with the army. Joash has stolen more than just your kinnor. He has stolen all your dreams. Life is unfair.

You despise Joash. With every year that goes by, you become more and more bitter. You grow up mean and grumpy.

THE END

You are so jealous that you can hardly bear to see Joash. Ignoring your jealous feelings, you take a deep breath and face him.

"My friend!" He greets you and gives you an enormous hug. He pulls you along after him and introduces you to so many soldiers that you can't remember all of their names.

Each person that you are introduced to says, "Sing for us." You are surprised at their request.

"I told them what a great singer you are," Joash says sheepishly.

"I thought you hated my singing."

Joash kicks the ground. "Actually, I was jealous of it."

"You were?"

"Yeah. I can hardly carry a tune. I'd really like it if you would sing for all of us. When you sing and worship God with your voice, I like the way it makes me feel. It's almost as if God is there, too."

You sing for them. They really seem to appreciate it, so you sing everything you know. They thank you when you are done. Days later when you see them marching out of the city, you are glad that you sang. You know they will need God's help.

When the army marches back into Jerusalem many days later, one of the Temple singers asks your parents if you can stay and work under him as his servant. He has heard the soldiers raving about your voice. Your parents agree. Both you and Joash

remain in Jerusalem, and you become lifelong
friends.

THE END

"I don't usually sing for people," you say, "but I'll try." You close your eyes and tell God, "I need your help to do this." Out loud, you say, "You almost carried me all the way home. Singing for you is the least I can do."

Simeon's warm smile encourages you.

You feel God's peace as you begin to play. You sing a psalm of praise that you learned from your father. When you finish singing, the house is quiet. You open your eyes. There are tears on your mother's cheeks. Your father's usually stern face has softened.

"Thank you," Simeon says. "That was beautiful. I feel refreshed."

You nod, a little embarrassed by his praise.

The next morning, the elders of your village gather to hear the king's message. Your father is in his best robes, and your mother has dabbed on a small amount of nard. She smells like sweet honey.

Simeon tells the village that King Jehoshaphat has called all of Judah to come to Jerusalem to fast and pray. The rumors are true. A huge attack is coming. Judah's enemies could strike any day.

The people of the village quickly pack food, clothing, and other necessities for the journey. Some are afraid to leave their valuables behind. They take everything they can carry. As you help your family pack, you remember how you fought the wolf. Somehow you feel braver than before. You wonder if you should stay behind to guard the village. You seldom miss with your slingshot.

CHOICE ONE: If you stay and protect your village, go to page 71.

CHOICE TWO: If you leave with your family, go to page 73.

The kinnor always brings you peace and comfort, and you want to play it. But what if your voice comes out squeaky like Joash said it does? You shake your head. "I'm sorry, but the dampness in the cave wasn't good for my voice. I think I should rest it. Perhaps another time."

Simeon smiles, "Of course."

You feel guilty about making excuses. You go for a walk, carrying your kinnor with you to a lonely spot near the edge of town. Sitting down where you do not think anyone will hear you, you begin to play and sing.

Instead of feeling peace, you feel ashamed. Just after you decide to go back and sing for Simeon, you feel Joash's arms around you again. He yanks your kinnor from your fingers. This time, you can't run after him. Your ankle hurts too much. You do not even try.

You limp home and help your parents prepare for the trip to Jerusalem. Your family leaves with a large group of others from the village.

One night on the way to Jerusalem, you go for a walk. Your ankle is feeling much better. You hear music in the distance. It sounds like some kind of harp. Quietly, you try to sneak up on whoever is playing it, not wanting to disturb the musician.

You hide behind a rock and peer around the edge of it. Joash is strumming your kinnor! You rush out. "What are you doing?" Joash stands up as if to flee. When you do not move closer, he stays where he is.

"I'm playing," he says defiantly.

This does not make sense, and you wonder for a minute if you are dreaming. Joash likes music? You want to say something mean to get back at him for taking your kinnor, but you recognize the embarrassment in his eyes.

Instead, you say, "Your playing sounded good, but I could teach you to play even better."

Joash looks at you uncertainly. Only the night breeze fills the silence between you until you say, "If you give me back my kinnor, we can find a place to practice every night."

"It'll be a secret, right?"

You nod. He gives you the kinnor with a sheepish smile. You hold it close to your chest.

"You're okay," he says.

"So are you," you say. "But why did you take so long to show it?"

He shrugs. You walk back to camp together.

THE END

"God of my fathers," you pray. "Please help me. If I don't die from bug bites, I'll eventually die from thirst and starvation." You feel God's peace settle on you and realize that you were panicking.

"Thank you, God," you say. Carefully, you twist your body to find a position where your ankle will not hurt. As you grab at the wall, your hand slips, and a rock tumbles over a ledge. It echoes as it hits bottom far below. You shiver. In the darkness, you try to concentrate on God's power instead of hairy spiders and dangerous pits.

Suddenly, you have an idea. You untie the sandal straps from around your ankle. Once the leather is released, you are able to gently slide your foot from beneath the rocks.

"Thank you, God," you say. Your foot hurts but you know you will be okay. Slowly you work the rough leather of your sandal free and tie it back onto your foot. A fine dust makes you sneeze.

You reach for a rock ledge on the wall to pull yourself up. As your hand slides onto it, you touch the edge of your kinnor. Your fingers quickly find the strings. Their gentle sound echoes in the passage. You realize that you would never have found your kinnor if your foot had not been wedged beneath the stones.

You wrap the kinnor in one of your arms and test your weight on your injured foot. You think you can work the kinks out of it. Limping, you slowly feel your way back to the entrance.

The light outside pierces your eyes. Shielding your face, you hobble as fast as you can back to your flock. When you reach them, a wolf leaps out, growling. It blocks your way to the sheep. You do not see Reuben anywhere.

CHOICE ONE: If you don't want to fight the wolf, go to page 56.

CHOICE TWO: If you attack the wolf, go to page 58.

"Help! Help!" you yell. No one hears you. You yell for hours. Your voice grows hoarse. You can barely hear your last, "Help!" before you decide to rest your voice.

You try to overcome your fear of the crawling creatures and lean against the wall. To find a more comfortable position, you pull yourself up and stretch your free leg. Your hand touches something that does not feel like a rock. It is your kinnor! You slide it off a ledge and hug it to yourself. It feels like you have found an old friend. You hold it up and begin to strum. Perhaps the music will float down the passage and draw someone in to investigate. You play it for some time, and the music comforts you.

"Is someone in there?" calls a deep voice.

"Yes. Help, I'm stuck," you yell as well as you can. Your voice cracks, "I'm over here." You play your instrument to guide him. A face appears in the shaft of light near the spider web.

"I'm Simeon," he says. He uses his staff as a lever to free your foot from the rocks.

As he helps you home, you find out that this important-looking man has a message for your town from King Jehoshaphat. You sneeze. Your head feels stuffy, you have a headache, and you feel a cough coming on.

"It was damp in that cave," Simeon says. "It's not really a good place to practice, you know."

You do not explain what you were doing in the cave. When you get home, you limp to the shelf where you usually keep the kinnor and put it away. You do not want to risk having Joash steal it again. It is too precious to you and your family. From now on, you will only make pipes out of reeds to play when you are watching the sheep. Joash has already broken two, but they are easy to make. You are a little disappointed that you will not be able to sing and play at the same time, but you will do anything you need to do to keep your family's kinnor safe.

THE END

A horror of dying washes over you.

"God is this true?" you ask. "Help me to know."

God has made you a singer, and the king has appointed you to go ahead of the army with the greatest singers in Judah. You do not want to die, but you know what you must do. Praising God is even better than defending your country. Whatever happens, you will march into battle for God and for Judah.

As you join the singers and begin the march toward the Desert of Tekoa and the enemy, your heart beats faster. Simeon's master gives a signal, and you all begin singing, "Give thanks to the Lord, for his love endures forever." Like King David of old, you are both a soldier and a singer. You are surprised that your dream has come true in a way that you could not have imagined.

The singing continues, louder and louder, as you approach the enemy camp. Suddenly, the singers in front of you halt. You move ahead of them to see why. As you sing, you stare down into the gorge where the enemy should be preparing to fight you. As far as you can see are enemy soldiers, thousands of them, but not one is standing. They are all dead. A loud cheer moves through the forces. You sing praises to God even louder than before.

God defeated Judah's enemies before your arrival! All that is left to do is to divide the enemy's things and take them home to your families. There is so much that it takes three days to gather it all. On the fourth day, you have a big praise party to thank God for his victory. Then you all march joyfully back to Jerusalem.

THE END

If Joash is telling the truth, then you will die.
You are afraid to die. You slip away from the
crowds and hide between the temporary camp and
Jerusalem's wall. You lean against the hard surface,
away from the squeeze of the crowd and the smell
of sweaty people.

When the singers pass through the gates, the
soldiers follow them. They look so majestic with all
of their weapons. You wish you had enough
courage to take part in that assembly. If only you
had not been chosen as one of Judah's sacrificial
lambs!

Then you notice that Joash is an arms bearer
for the soldiers. He sees you and smirks.

At that moment, you know he was lying.
Jehaziel's words come back to you. God said that
Judah would win the battle. How could you have
forgotten that, even for a second? If you had taken
your place up front with the singers, you would
have seen God's victory first-hand. How could you
have been such a fool? You vow never to let your
fears rule your life again. You walk back to where
your family is staying.

Eventually, the battle is won, and the fast is
over. But not even your mother's bread satisfies
you. You regret your cowardly decision for the rest
of your life.

THE END

The wolf slinks toward the flock. Your rod, sling, and scrip full of stones lie nearby. You can't let the wolf kill one of your sheep. You put down the kinnor and grab your rod. Ignoring the throbbing in your injured foot, you chase after the wolf. Suddenly, you slip and twist your ankle again. The pain causes you to drop the rod, and it falls to the ground. The wolf snarls at you, and then it bolts after an old ewe.

You've chased off many wolves before, but you are in too much pain to do it now. You can't think straight. You decide to go find help. You ignore the urgent bleats of your frightened sheep. Passing the carcass of a dead lamb, you start for home.

You hear Reuben calling from the other side of the pasture. "Use your sling!"

You think there might be more than one wolf. Your mind is confused by the pain you are feeling. You can't find your sling. Reuben needs more help than what you can give him.

"I'm going for Father," you shout.

By the time your father reaches the flock, four sheep have been killed. Only later do you realize your mistake. You quit instead of staying to help Reuben any way you could. You feel awful.

By the next day, the whole town is talking about you. They laugh when Joash tells them how you bragged about fighting off enemy troops. He says, "The braggart couldn't even chase away an old wolf with one eye and three legs."

Joash is lying about the wolf, which had all its parts, but you hang your head anyway. Everyone thinks you are a coward. Soldiers can't be cowards. You give up on your dream of ever helping to save Judah from the enemy. You remain a shepherd for the rest of your life.

THE END

You see your rod on the ground not far away.
You keep eye contact with the wolf as you edge
closer to it. The wolf snarls, as if ready to pounce.
Its coarse, gray hide bristles as it creeps closer. The
sheep are bleating and bumping into each other.
Your rod is almost within reach. You pray that
Reuben will arrive soon.

You lunge for your rod, and then roll toward
the beast. Swinging it across the ground, you trip
the wolf. It lets out a whimper. You spring to your
feet and ignore the pain of your throbbing ankle.
Before the wolf can recover, you land a solid blow
to its head. It goes limp, but you hit it again and
again.

You hear Reuben's voice behind you. "I think
it's dead." You stop hitting the beast but keep your
rod poised in case it moves.

When it does not move, you throw your rod
away from you. "It was attacking the sheep."

Reuben smiles. "You were unbelievable! That
animal has terrorized the flocks around here for
days. This will make you a hero."

A man you do not know is standing a few feet
behind Reuben. Did he see everything? You feel
blood rising to your face and give Reuben a ques-
tioning look.

"This is Simeon. I met him on the way here.
He's got a message from the king for our town. I
thought you could take him to see the elders."

"Sure," you say. Suddenly your foot gives out, and you drop to the ground.

"You're hurt," Reuben says.

"A little."

Reuben and Simeon wrap your foot with cloth while you tell them about Joash and your kinnor. You tie the kinnor to your chest.

"You've had quite a day," Simeon says. "Why don't you lean on me?" He puts an arm around your waist. You begin hobbling toward the village.

"What does King Jehoshaphat want to say to us?" you ask.

"Everyone must go to Jerusalem, because our enemies are about to attack," Simeon says. "Here lean this way. It might be easier."

So the rumors are true. The little bumps and gullies on the path feel a lot deeper now.

Simeon continues, "Reuben tells me that you sing and play the kinnor. I'd love to hear it."

You smile but do not answer. It is one thing to sing for God and the sheep. The thought of singing for a stranger, especially a king's messenger, makes you tremble. You pretend to concentrate on walking. Simeon seems to understand and remains quiet. When you get to your house, he tells your parents about the king's message.

"You must stay with us," your mother says.

"Thank you for your hospitality," Simeon replies with a smile.

It would be hard for any visitor to turn down your mother's invitation, especially with the smell of bread fresh in the air.

After supper, Simeon asks again, "Would you play the kinnor and let me hear you sing?"

You are tired, and your ankle is throbbing. You really do not feel like singing.

CHOICE ONE: If you sing for Simeon, go to page 45.

CHOICE TWO: If you do not sing, go to page 47.

You head for Jerusalem. Although you don't know the exact route, you know the general direction. You travel as quickly as you can.

As you near Jerusalem, you are surprised at how many people are in the city. You even see friends from your village, and you find your parents.

"I am so sorry for running away," you tell them as they hug you.

"We should have believed you," they say. They hand you the kinnor. "When you left, Joash told the truth and brought this back."

You go to see the king. When you report to the king's ministers what you have seen and heard, you are surprised to learn that God has already spoken to the king about the foreign armies. Again, you are amazed at God's lovingkindness. As you are leaving the palace, you can't help but break out in song.

The next morning, a messenger from King Jehoshaphat wakes your family. "Please forgive the early hour," he says, "but the king has heard your child singing." He turns to you. "The king wants to reward your courage by having you join the Temple singers as they lead the army into battle today."

You smile. "I would like that. Where do I go?"

In the pale light of dawn, the servant leads you through the streets to the front of the ranks. Instead of soldiers, musicians are leading the way. You recognize some of them as Korahites and Kohathites, Temple singers like your great-grandfather, who played your kinnor decades before you. As the march to battle begins, you are in awe of the other singers. You realize what an honor it is to serve God as a musician. You discover that there are many ways to fight for Judah. One of the best ways is to worship God in song. You march boldly forward as a warrior, a singing warrior.

God has already done many miraculous things for you and for your country. You can't wait to see his awesome power at work today.

THE END

You walk toward your village, or where you think your village might be, since you are not sure where you are. Because of the number of times that you lose your way, it takes you an entire day to reach home.

The village looks strange when you first walk into it. There are no people outside of their homes, no animal noises, no laughter. The streets are deserted. Even the herds are gone.

You hurry to your house. No one is home. It appears as though everyone left in a hurry. You do not know what to do.

You scrounge around for some food to make a meal for yourself and fall asleep on your bed. Over the next few days, you spend most of the time eating and sleeping. You become bored.

One day, two enemy soldiers come to town. They recognize you as the crazy child that visited their camp, and they start laughing again. They leave you alone. They do not stay long. You go from one house to the next and try to take care of the things that your neighbors forgot to do.

Finally after days and days, your family returns. You are overjoyed to see them, and they are thrilled to see you. Joash has told the truth and returned the kinnor to your father.

As you sit down to the first decent meal in days, your family tells you about how Judah's army defeated the foreigners. You are amazed. You tell them about your time in the enemies' camp and about what happened there. They laugh at your story. You can see that they do not believe you, not completely. But you don't care. You know the truth, and it does not matter what other people think of you anymore. God cares for you. He proved it by saving you from enemy soldiers—twice! That is enough for you.

THE END

You enter the cave on the left and move forward cautiously. Something flies over your head and disappears outside. You hear other movement, and wonder what kinds of creatures live in the cave. You hear a high-pitched whistle, and your lamp blows out.

Shaking, you tell yourself that the wind can't hurt you. And all those other sounds you hear are just your imagination. You run your hands along the cave's wall to find your way and continue down the passage.

Just as you are about ready to give up, your hand catches a sticky spider web. You try to shake it loose, which causes you to trip and fall into something slimy. Your elbow hits a sharp stone.

"Ouch! That Joash! I'll get him yet!" you yell to boost your courage. As you pull yourself up, your hand touches a smooth object. You touch it again and hear the faint sound of musical strings vibrating.

"I found it!" you say. You can't believe it. You hug the kinnor to your body and retrace your steps back to the cave entrance and then home.

In the morning, you show your parents the kinnor.

"I'm glad you found it," your father says. "Please be more careful from now on."

Your mother notices a few new scratches on the instrument.

The scratches look more like grooves to you.

You can feel your anger rising. You want to get back at Joash for hurting your instrument. You know you are too small to fight him. You would not stand a chance.

Later, you take the kinnor to your secret place outside the village. You sit down inside a group of large stones where no one can see or hear you. There you pour out your frustration to God in song, just as King David did. When you go back to the village, you find out that King Jehoshaphat has called all of Judah to Jerusalem. Enemies will attack soon.

Your whole village packs up and heads for Jerusalem. You take your kinnor on the journey. That evening, you sing for the people to keep up spirits and quiet fears. Soon other townspeople sing with you, even Joash. You do not mind. You, Joash, and all the rest of the people are in this together.

THE END

You climb down into the cave on your right. You do not have to wait long for your eyes to get used to the darkness, since you came into it from the night. The lamp lights your way. You hold it out in front of you and search every crevice for your kinnor.

After some time, the cave narrows down to nothing. You have searched most of the night and have not found what you came for. You return home. If you get a good night's rest, perhaps you can go back tomorrow night to search the other cave. You lie down on your mat, exhausted.

All too soon, your mother is shaking you. "Wake up! We have to pack."

King Jehoshaphat has sent messengers all over Judah. Everyone has to meet with him in Jerusalem.

You do not want your kinnor to wait in a cave until you return. The dampness will ruin it, but you can't go looking for it until you get back. You are so angry with Joash that you find him on the streets of your village.

"You traitor! You Ammonite!" You push his shoulder as hard as you can and then hit him.

Joash is surprised by your attack. You have never had the nerve to fight him before. You lunge at him again before he can say anything. Your anger makes you stronger. And without his buddies, Joash does not seem so powerful.

Within moments, though, he gets angry and

starts fighting back. He punches you, and your stomach feels as if it has been pushed up to your throat. As you wrestle to the ground, you hear your tunic ripping.

"Stop this, both of you!" You feel strong arms pulling you and Joash apart.

"I didn't start it," complains Joash. You are surprised at how little he looks next to his father.

"People of Judah should live together in peace," his father says. "We'll be fighting foreigners soon enough. Come, Son. We have to get ready to leave." Joash looks back at you as they walk away. He does not look as mean as before.

You walk home. You feel bile rise to your mouth from your stomach and can't seem to get rid of that bitter taste. You feel like you could throw up.

Your father meets you at the door. "Why aren't you packing? You should be getting ready to leave." You know he is distracted, because he does not notice your torn tunic.

"I'm sorry," you say. Joash's father's words trouble you. You ask, "Are we really going to have a war?"

"Yes." He hurries away to prepare so that you can leave immediately. You help your mother and brother pack.

Later, Joash comes to your house. "Here." He thrusts your kinnor at you and then disappears. You think it might be his way of apologizing.

"I'm sorry, too!" you call after him.

As you close the door, you remember what his father said, "People of Judah should live together in peace." You decide that if you get through this war alive, you will try to make friends with Joash.

THE END

When your family starts to leave, you tell your father, "Someone should guard the village."

He shakes his head no. "The king has summoned us. We need to obey. God will watch over our town."

You know you should listen to your father, but hiding in Jerusalem is for cowards, not for heroes. As the whole town heads toward Jerusalem, you slip farther and farther behind until you reach the end of the group. You dart behind a boulder and hide until the bleating of sheep and barking of dogs have faded away.

You are glad you planned ahead and brought your scrip. You fill it with smooth stones for the battle you expect to come. The only sound you hear is the scraping of your leather sandals on the dirt road. The cloud-filled sky seems to grow angry and the rock-speckled hills lose their friendliness. Maybe you can catch up with the others. You turn around to run after them, but then you remember Joash's taunting. He would call you a coward. You continue toward the village.

The deserted town has taken on a new darkness. You had no idea that silence could beat so loudly against your ears. You scrounge for food. Everything you find is cold and tastes moldy. You curl up on your mat. It feels even harder than usual as you wait for daybreak with your rod at your side.

The next morning is sunny, and you set up a

watch just outside of town. It feels odd to be on watch without the sheep. All the animals are with your family. The days seem longer now, especially because you can't sing to pass the time. That would give away your position.

You know you are drifting from God—you hardly even think of him anymore—but you don't have the energy to think about that. You have to take care of yourself.

One afternoon, you are sitting on a rock watching the horizon. Everything looks so wavy in the heat that it almost makes you dizzy. You lean over to get a drink of water from the animal skin in the shade by your feet. Suddenly two strong arms grab you from behind. They feel like iron bands around your chest. You try to wrestle free, but soon find yourself on the ground with a knife pressed against your throat. Angry, dark eyes stare into yours. You realize that your assailant is an Ammonite spy. You wonder how he was able to get past your watch.

"Where are the people of this town?" he demands.

"What town?" you say.

He kills you for being a smart aleck.

THE END

You leave with your family for Jerusalem. Your ankle heals fairly quickly, since it was just a slight sprain. Your family is traveling with others from your village for protection from bandits and wild animals. You try to avoid Joash and his friends, but you have to help keep your family's sheep moving in the right direction. Sometimes the bullies fall back to where you are just to taunt you.

You arrive at Jerusalem without incident, but the king has called a fast for all of Judah. You hate going hungry, but Judah needs God's help. People from all the towns have come to fast and pray. From what you have heard, only a miracle can save your country now.

Simeon finds your family at the camp your town has set up inside the city walls. You welcome him into your tent as a friend but are surprised at his words.

"I'd like you to sing for my master, one of the Temple singers."

When Simeon tells you the man's name, your mother says, "He's a distant cousin. Like you, he is a Kohathite descendant of Levi."

You are not sure what to say.

"It would be an honor to sing for this man," your father says. It was his gentle way of telling you that you should go with Simeon. All you can think about is your growling stomach. You feel a little faint.

"Your music gave me such peace from God," says Simeon. "Won't you please allow my master that same peace?"

"I think you should do it," your mother says. "But it's your choice."

CHOICE ONE: If you sing for Simeon's master, go to page 83.

CHOICE TWO: If you do not sing for Simeon's master, go to page 86.

"I was kicked out," you say and try to look as dejected as possible. "No one in Judah wants me around."

"Why did you run from us then?" asks a man.

"I run from everyone," you say. "I am not liked by others." You know you are lying, but you think the man believes you. "I am an orphan. No one wanted another mouth to feed. I have lived on my own in the wilderness for many years."

The man talks quietly to the others. You know you look disheveled. You think they are discussing whether or not your story is true, but they are talking so fast that you can only understand a few words. You try not to act like you are interested.

Finally, the man says, "Come with me." You follow him, not knowing if they believed you or not. You walk through the entire camp, and it takes a long time. There are thousands of soldiers. You wonder if Judah has any chance at all against so many. You pass tent after tent and see swords and spears everywhere.

At the end of the camp is a caravan.

"You are now my slave, the slave of Hazzan," the soldier says. He gives instructions to the caravan. You are chained to a camel. You walk for days. Finally, when you think your legs can't move another step, you reach a large house. It is your new master's house, Hazzan's house.

You do not get to sleep in the big house, but in

the stable. It smells of animal waste. Your job is to feed and care for the pigs. You get to eat whatever slop they leave, and that isn't much. After all, they eat like pigs. You grow used to the fermented, mildewed, and muddy tastes of your meals. You wait for your master to return, but he never does. You wonder why.

THE END

You know that they won't believe you, but you tell your whole story anyway. You tell how Joash stole your kinnor and then lied about it. You tell how your parents reacted, and how hurt that made you feel.

"I ran away. I ran most of the night." While you are speaking, you are sorry for not waiting at home for the truth to come out. It usually does. You know your parents love you, and you wish you had never left.

Knowing that this is probably the last time that you will be given a chance to speak before they kill you, you decide to tell the enemy soldiers what you really think of them.

You say, "The God of Judah is all powerful, mightier than you and all of your false gods put together. You can't hurt me unless my God lets you. If he wanted to, he could help me fight all of you at once, and I would win."

The men throw back their heads and roar with laughter. You stand proudly waiting for death, but no one takes you seriously. They think you are crazy. They give you lukewarm water and stale bread, and then they let you go.

As you stand outside the foreigner's camp, you thank God for saving your life. It astonishes you that he would care for you even after you ran away in anger.

CHOICE ONE: If you head for Jerusalem to warn King Jehoshaphat about the enemy army, go to page **62.**

CHOICE TWO: If you head back to your village, go to page **64.**

You nod and follow him. The slave leads you around the back part of the camp and into a small tent.

"This is where I stay," he says. "You will be safe here until dark."

"Why are you helping me?" you ask.

"I have been a slave all of my life," he says. "If they find you, they will make you a slave, too. I would not wish my hard life on anyone."

You nod. "Thank you."

"There's food over there," he says before he disappears.

You wait in the small tent alone. You try to stay alert in case of trouble, but your long run yesterday wore you out. By afternoon, you fall asleep.

Just before dawn of the next day, the slave wakes you.

"It is time," he says. You follow him out of the tent and to the edge of the camp. He leads you to a path that is barely visible in the early morning light.

Just after you pass some large rocks, two men smelling like camel dung grab you. They hold your wrists together in a tight grasp.

"This is the spy," the boy says. "I want my silver."

"What are you doing?" you yell.

A hand comes over your mouth and presses in until you taste filth. Now you are sure the smell was camel dung. You gag and want to spit the horrible flavor out.

"If you make another sound," says a rough voice, "I won't be so nice." You are really scared.

Someone tosses the slave a coin. "Now get out of here before I decide to take you with me as a slave, too."

"Humph," says the slave. He turns to you. "It isn't personal. With this money, I can buy my freedom. Anyway, being a slave is better than being dead. I saved your life." He turns and leaves. The men carry you to the other side of the ridge. Waiting for them is a small caravan.

You travel to Egypt and live there as a slave for the rest of your life.

THE END

You don't trust the boy, but you nod. He moves away from you, and you follow. As soon as you have your footing and his back is turned, you break into a run.

Within seconds, you hear him shouting, "Enemy spy! Enemy spy!" Almost immediately, you hear the thud of feet running behind you. They are gaining on you, but you do not look back.

Vice-like hands grab you from behind. They jerk you to a halt. You are out of breath and coughing. They half-carry and half-drag you back to their camp.

You are thrown on the ground in front of a high-ranking soldier. He pulls you by your hair to a kneeling position and makes you face him. He smells like strange spices, but they don't cover up the fact that he probably has not had a bath in years. You wish he would move one step away from you.

"You seem too young to be a spy. Are you the best that Judah can do?"

CHOICE ONE: If you tell him that you are an outcast from Judah, go to page 75.

CHOICE TWO: If you tell him that you ran away from your parents, go to page 77.

You nod. You can't even find your voice to agree. You almost wish that you had never played for Simeon in the first place.

That evening, you are brought to the outer courtyard of the great Temple to sing before Simeon's master. Before you begin, you wipe your hands on your tunic and wonder how cold hands can sweat. You tremble as you hold the kinnor and position your fingers over the strings. Simeon's master smiles to encourage you. You are afraid to look at him, so you close your eyes and try to sing just to God. The distant smell of incense helps remind you that God is near. You sing of God's victory against the Egyptians.

As you finish, you notice that the courtyard is silent. You open your eyes to see why. A man is watching you. Everyone else is bowing. It's King Jehoshaphat! You stand up and bow, too, almost dropping the kinnor. When you look up again, the king is gone.

"Thank you," Simeon's master says. He gives you a cool drink of water. You feel it hit the bottom of your empty stomach. All the people are gathering outside of the Temple to hear King Jehoshaphat.

"Stay with me," Simeon says, "so you won't get lost in this crowd." You tie your kinnor around your waist and keep close to him.

All of Judah is there when Jehoshaphat stands up to speak. Instead of giving a speech he prays,

"O Lord, God of our fathers, are you not the God who is in heaven? You rule over all the kingdoms of the nations. Power and might are in your hand, and no one can withstand you."

The king prays a long time. He finishes with, "O our God, will you not judge them? For we have no power to face this vast army that is attacking us. We do not know what to do, but our eyes are upon you."

All the people pray with him, but silently. You had no idea that the enemy was so strong. Even the king is afraid. A man stands up suddenly. Simeon tells you that his name is Jahaziel.

"Listen, King Jehoshaphat and all who live in Judah and Jerusalem!" he says. This is what the Lord says to you: 'Do not be afraid or discouraged because of this vast army. For the battle is not yours, but God's....'"

When he finishes speaking, Jehoshaphat bows down to worship the Lord with his face to the ground. Everyone else does the same, including you. Suddenly, some Levites stand up and start shouting, praising God as loudly as they can. You feel God's power and can't help but stand up and join in, waving your arms in the air.

You wake up early the next morning, anxious for God's battle to begin. As the soldiers are about to leave, Jehoshaphat decides to have singers lead the way, praising the great and holy Lord. You are standing with Simeon as his master is chosen.

"And you will sing, too," King Jehoshaphat says. You look up to see him pointing right at you! You smile in acknowledgement of his words. You are overjoyed, as the king leaves.

Someone sidles up to you and whispers in your ear. "Better you than me." It is Joash.

"What do you mean? It's a great honor."

"No, I'd call it a great strategy. The king knows that the enemy will be tired of killing singers before they ever get to the soldiers. It will give Judah the advantage."

Joash gives you a tight hug. He appears sincere when he says, "Thank you for sacrificing yourself for the good of your people."

Before you can answer, he walks away.

CHOICE ONE: If you join the singers, go to page 53.

CHOICE TWO: If you do not join the singers, go to page 55.

You think about singing in public. What if the soldiers heard you? You would look like a sissy to the bravest men of Judah.

"Thank you, Simeon," you say, "but I would rather wait until I can eat again. I don't want the rumblings of my stomach to drown out my singing." Everyone laughs.

"Perhaps you can train your stomach to keep time to the music," Reuben says.

Simeon is gracious. "My master would appreciate hearing you whenever you're ready. Thank you."

You feel bad about turning Simeon down, so you offer to walk partway home with him. The crowded city teams with voices. The odor of animal dung stings your nostrils. You hear some loud praying. Through open tent flaps, you hear children whining for food in chorus with the bleating of sheep and goats in their makeshift pens. You notice that a large group of soldiers have camped together. You stop. Simeon sees your interest and suggests that you visit. He introduces you to a guard before he leaves.

"Interested in soldiering, are you?" the guard asks, chuckling. "Go ahead and take a look around."

As you pick your way through the area, some soldiers smile at you. Many are praying and do not notice you at all. Others stare into space. You won-

der if soldiers get just as scared as everyone else.
Two soldiers are talking by an unlit fire pit. You
join them.

"Can you believe it?" the older soldier says.
"Isaac is sick. I don't think he'll be able to march
into battle with us."

"You'll have to carry all your weapons yourself," another says. He has a scar on his cheek.

Your ears perk up. Maybe you could be the
man's arms bearer for the battle! "Excuse me, but I
would be happy to help," you say. "I know I'm
small, but I'm strong. And I'm a deadeye with a
sling."

The men appear amused, as if they think you
are joking. Finally, the man with the scar puts his
face right up to yours. "Prove it."

You never go anywhere without your sling, so
you pull it from the girdle tied around your waist.

"See that jar over there?" You point to an earth-
enware jar at the far side of the camp. You load a
smooth stone into the sling, swing, aim, and fire.
The jar shatters.

"You have a job." The older man said. "My
name is Enan. When the time comes, you will
march into battle at my side.

When you tell your parents, your mother looks
worried. Your father says, "Maybe this will help you
get this idea of soldiering out of your system. Do
what you're asked to do and you'll be fine."

Your mother harrumphs. "I'll be praying that Isaac has a miraculous recovery."

The day arrives for the soldiers to leave. As you march in the midst of Judah's army, you feel like an ant in tall grass. The soldiers look so fierce! It takes all your courage just to stay with them. You are near the back of the column of soldiers. Then after all of your walking, Enan does not even get to the battle before it is over. You are not sure who was killed or who fought, but you help him pick up the spoils from the enemy. When you return to Jerusalem, Enan gives you some of the spoils—the things you took from the enemy camp—to bring to your parents. Your family is thankful for the many fine things that you bring to them. Enan's arms bearer is well again, so you help your parents get ready for the trip home.

THE END

You don't want to be responsible for losing your family's kinnor. You decide never to play it around Joash again. When Reuben relieves you, you hurry home to have a good cry.

Your father greets you at the door. "Hurry to the Rabbi's house with your kinnor. A king's messenger has arrived. I volunteered you to sing for him. Gideon's sending his son over, too."

"You mean Joash?"

Your father nods. When you arrive, Joash looks as upset as you feel. You try to hide your kinnor behind a leg of the Rabbi's table.

"Boys, why don't you sing King David's first psalm?" the Rabbi asks. You begin. You are amazed at how well your voices blend together.

When you are done, the messenger says, "Excellent! Would you sing again and play your kinnor this time?"

You steal a glance at Joash. He looks from you to the messenger. Without a word, he brings your instrument to you.

"Thanks," you say. You both smile. From that day forward you live together in perfect harmony.

THE END

You become angrier and angrier about Joash's bullying. For the rest of the day, you try to think of a way to make Joash pay for what he did to you. You hide behind a rock near his house, waiting for your opportunity.

"Joash," his mother calls. "I'm leaving the soup on the fire. Stay here and watch it until I get back. Stir it every few minutes so it won't burn."

"Sure," says Joash, but as soon as his mother is out of sight, he pulls the pot away from the fire and runs to his friend's house. Quickly, you grab two handfuls of dirt, dump them into the soup, and push the pot over the highest flames. You run back to your hiding place. Joash returns and stares at the pot, confused. His mother walks in just as he starts stirring.

She takes one look at the soup and begins to shriek. "It's burnt!" She tastes it and spits out the food into a cloth. "What have you done? You have ruined our evening meal." She grabs him by the ear. "This is the last prank you will ever pull."

Joash looks dumbfounded. "But I did what you said."

You smile. If he admits to leaving, he will get in trouble for disobeying. If he says he stayed, he will be blamed for the spoiled soup. Your job is done. "It serves him right," you think.

Soon your gloating is swept aside when you hear the report from a messenger. "King

Jehoshaphat is calling all of Judah to Jerusalem."

After the announcement, your family hurries home to pack. You find your broken staff just outside the door.

"How did Joash know I did it?" you wonder. As you tie bundles of clothes and food, you plan how to get even with Joash for breaking your staff.

That is how your life goes from then on. You and Joash keep harming each other. Nothing is as important to you as being one-up on Joash. You lead a miserable life.

THE END

You quickly close the tent flap and try to hide under the covering you used the night before. The noise and killing continue outside. There seems to be no end to it. You try to eat the leftover bread from your master's breakfast, but it tastes stale.

Suddenly your master stumbles into the tent. He has been stabbed. You try to stay hidden, but he sees you.

"Come here, child," he says.

Perhaps he will give you your freedom now. Cautiously, you inch toward him, keeping the doorway in view. Blood is pouring from his wound.

"I am dying," he says.

You can't help but ask, "Now do you believe in the power of Judah's God?"

"Judah's God? What has your God to do with it?"

You think his answer is odd.

He grabs your arm with a bloody hand. "If I have to die, so do you." Before you can get away, he stabs you. You die on the floor of the tent beside him.

THE END

You shut the goat hair flap and pray for
courage. Then you hurry to the shaded side of the
tent. You have been working a section of it loose
for days, every moment that you were left alone.
You lift up the bottom edge and slide underneath it,
scraping against the ground as you do it. You are
outside.

Shadows are still deep on this side of the tent.
You silently race from the shadow of one tent to the
shadow of the next tent. Several times you must
wait for fighting to stop and your escape route to
clear.

Sometimes you have to scurry over fallen bodies to reach the next shadow. Three tents left to
pass. Two tents. One tent. As soon as you pass the
last tent, you are in sunlight. You enjoy the warmth
of it on your face.

You take off at a run, hoping that the soldiers
are too busy fighting to notice you. The noise of
battle, metal on metal, and the groans of the dying
fade behind you. You press on, ignoring the sharp
rocks cutting into your feet through the holes in
your sandals.

You reach a small rise of ground with a protec-
tive rock outcropping. You slide behind the rocks
and hold your stomach to catch your breath.

From your vantage point, you can see the
whole camp. It is strewn with bodies. Where is
Judah? King Jehoshaphat's soldiers are not even

there! The Ammonites and Moabites have killed all the men from Mount Seir. Now they are killing each other!

"This has to be the work of God," you say out loud. "God made Judah's enemies turn on themselves!"

Before too long, all is silent. The breeze no longer brings you the occasional sound of dying men. Your mouth is dry, but you don't leave the rocks to find water. In the distance, you hear a loud, musical sound. Who could it be? Now you can see an army marching toward the foreigner's camp.

You listen closely. The noise is music. You recognize the words. You recognize Judah's army. Judah is singing praises to God!

You shake your head. Your God is even more amazing than you thought. You raise your voice and worship God in song.

THE END

Attack!

Spiritual Building Block: **Obedience**

You can do the following things to better know and follow God's will:

Think About It:

What do you want to do with your life? Do you have grand plans and great goals? God planted those passions in your heart, and he gave you the ability to be able to do it. On the other hand, if you're not quite sure what you will do when you grow up, that's okay. It's great to be open to different ideas that God might give you. Either way, make sure to spend time in prayer, asking the Holy Spirit to direct your steps.

Talk About It:

Sometimes it is hard to obey. Some of the things God or parents or teachers or even presidents ask us to do are really hard. Lots of Christians struggle with this issue. Find a pastor or a parent or Christian friend to talk to about how you feel. God wants us to be real with him. Only then will you be able to obey him with joy.

Try It:

If you want God to trust you with the big stuff, you have to be able to handle the little stuff. That means: obey your parents, do the nitty-gritty of homework and chores well and with a good attitude, be kind even to your little sister, listen to good advice. Those kinds of things. God will reward you. And you will be much happier.

COLLECT THEM ALL!

DEADLY EXPEDITION!

Imagine that your decisions determine whether you will ever enter the Promised Land.

You and your entire nation of Hebrew slaves have just escaped from the Egyptians and are heading toward the land that God has promised to give you. But when you reach the Red Sea, you look behind to see the entire Egyptian army closing in on you! You must make a choice. Will you stand and fight the Egyptian army? Or will you trust God and miraculously cross the sea on a dry path—only to face the possibility of battling yet another nation? You must make a choice.

ESCAPE!

Imagine that your decisions have the power to determine the fate of many Christians.

You have become a believer of Jesus Christ—even though you know you might die because of it. You see one of your favorite Christians, Stephen, being dragged off by temple officials to be killed for his faith. You must make a choice. You run off to warn your family that danger is coming. As you are leaving, you overhear people making plans to raid the home of your good friends. You must make a choice.

TRAPPED!

Imagine that your decisions have the power to determine whether your family will be saved from its enemies.

Your Aunt Rahab is one of your favorite people, but your father doesn't want you to spend time with her. You must make a choice. When you visit her house you discover that the enemy of your people has been using her house as a hide-out! You must make a choice. Do you listen to Rahab's reasons for helping the spies? Do you believe her when she says that you must stay with her to be safe? Not everyone in your family believes her. You must make a choice.